John Morris

The Venerable Sir Adrian Fortescue

Knight of the bath, knight of St. John, martyr

John Morris

The Venerable Sir Adrian Fortescue
Knight of the bath, knight of St. John, martyr

ISBN/EAN: 9783337298876

Printed in Europe, USA, Canada, Australia, Japan

Cover: Foto ©Raphael Reischuk / pixelio.de

More available books at **www.hansebooks.com**

THE VENERABLE

SIR ADRIAN FORTESCUE

KNIGHT OF THE BATH, KNIGHT OF ST. JOHN

MARTYR

BY

FATHER JOHN MORRIS, S.J.

LONDON

BURNS AND OATES, Limited

———

1887

The Venerable Adrian Fortescue, Martyr.

AMONGST the Martyrs of the time of Henry the Eighth, who were not depicted on the walls of the English College Church and who are therefore not included in the Decree that gave to fifty-four Martyrs the honours of the Blessed, are three Knights of the Order of St. John of Jerusalem. These are Sir Adrian Fortescue and Sir Thomas Dingley, who were beheaded on Tower Hill on the 8th or 10th of July, 1539, and Sir David Gunston, who was hanged, drawn, and quartered at St. Thomas Waterings in Southwark on July 1, 1541. Of these three Martyrs hardly a word has been published by Catholic writers, excepting that Fortescue and Dingley were attainted by Act of Parliament for denying the King's Supremacy ; and that Gunston was tried and found guilty of high treason for the same cause. Of Sir Thomas Dingley and Sir David Gunston there is little more, as yet, that can be said ; but fortunately modern research, and more especially the labours of Thomas (Fortescue) Lord Clermont, the historian of his family, have put us in possession of a considerable body of information respecting Sir Adrian Fortescue. He comes of an interesting family, of which Lord Clermont modestly says that it is "a fair example of a knightly and noble house of England," and it will be well for us under his guidance to learn something, not only of our Martyr, but of those who went before him and followed after him of his blood and name.

The family tradition is that amongst the warriors in the host of William the Conqueror was the Duke's cup-bearer, Richard le Fort, who at the Battle of Hastings, when his master's horse was killed under him, saved his life by the shelter of his "strong shield." Fort or Forz he is named in the Rolls of Battle Abbey, but henceforward he was called Fort-Escu ; and in reference to this event his modern descendants have taken for their motto *Forte scutum salus ducum*, "A strong shield the safety of leaders." Richard Fort-Escu returned to Normandy, where his line was

B

continued through his second son and lasted for seven centuries. In England his eldest son, Sir Adam, became the recipient of the Conqueror's bounties, having various grants of land made to him. His seat was at Wimstone in South Devon, and he is the ancestor of all the English Fortescues. His descendants were in succession a second and third Adam and then a William; in the next generation the eldest son was Sir John, and the other two sons, Sir Richard and Sir Nicholas, Knights of St. John, who fought in the Holy Land under Richard Cœur de Lion. The line of the eldest sons was continued by a Sir Richard, three more Adams, and four Williams. With the last of these, who was married in 1394, our interest in the main line of the family ceases, for his brother Sir John, who in 1422 was Governor of Meaux in France, is the ancestor of the branch of the family with which we are concerned. He had three sons: the eldest, Sir Henry, was Lord Chief Justice of Common Pleas in Ireland in 1426; the second was Sir John, the famous Chancellor Fortescue, from whom Earl Fortescue and Lord Clermont descend; and the third Sir Richard, who was killed at the Battle of St. Alban's in 1455. The youngest of these three distinguished men was the grandfather of the Venerable Adrian Fortescue.

We have not paused to mention points of interest connected with these ancestors of our Martyr, as that Sir John, his great-grandfather, fought at Agincourt. But we cannot pass in silence the Chancellor, Sir John Fortescue, Sir Adrian's great-uncle, one of whose legal works he has converted into a relic by transcribing it with his own hand. The title by which he is best known is that of Chancellor, but it was in the office of Lord Chief Justice of England, which he held for eighteen years, that his high legal reputation was made. To this he was appointed in 1442, when he was forty-six or forty-eight years old, and he had then been King's Serjeant twelve years and a law student some sixteen years before that. We may presume from the general use of the title that he really was Lord Chancellor of England. He certainly had held the title of that office when he was in exile with Henry the Sixth, whose fortunes he shared; but he was still Chief Justice when he fought by Henry's side on Palm Sunday, 1461. On the utter overthrow of the Lancastrians at the bloody Battle of Towton, he withdrew to Durham and afterwards to Edinburgh in attendance on King Henry, Queen Margaret, and the Prince of Wales. The Chancellor of the

Prince he had long been. He was attainted by Edward the Fourth's first Parliament, which was not wonderful, seeing that at the same time the last three sovereigns were declared to be usurpers. Sir John remained in Scotland with King Henry, using his pen and his legal intellect in his behalf; and when Edward made Henry his prisoner in 1465, the Chancellor accompanied Queen Margaret and the Prince when they fled to the Continent. For nearly six years his life was spent in teaching the Prince of Wales, and in writing political letters in his fallen master's service. Henry the Sixth, who had been freed from the Tower by Clarence and Warwick, after six months of liberty was made prisoner once more after the Battle of Barnet on Easter Sunday, 1471; and on that very Easter Sunday the Queen and Prince Edward, with the Chancellor, landed at Weymouth. The Battle of Tewkesbury followed on the 4th of May, and there the Prince was killed, the Queen was taken, and among the prisoners was Sir John Fortescue. King Henry was murdered in the Tower on the 21st of May, and there was no one left but Edward the Fourth to claim the aged lawyer's allegiance. In October, 1471, under the Broad Seal, and with the assent of Parliament Edward granted Sir John Fortescue a pardon, but before his lands were restored to him the King required that he should write an answer to his own arguments against Edward's title to the realm of England. He did what was required of him with much *bonhommie*, like a man who had been accustomed to defend a cause for a fee, and in February, 1474, when he was eighty years old, he got his answer *Soit fait come il desire*. At this time he wrote his treatise *On Absolute and Limited Monarchy*, the copy of which in the Bodleian, in his great-nephew's handwriting, bearing the date of 1532, was published in 1714 by Lord Fortescue of Credan; and he left other works, of which the best known is his book in praise of the laws of England. The exact date of his death is not known.

We have said that Sir John Fortescue, the Governor of Meaux, had three sons, of which the Chancellor was the second. We are now concerned with the third, Sir Richard, who was our martyr's grandfather, called "of Punsborne," from his estate. His life was lost in 1455 at the Battle of St. Alban's, near his own residence of Punsborne, the first conflict between Henry the Sixth and the Yorkists. Sir Richard, like his brother the Chancellor, took King Henry's part in this fratricidal War of the Roses. He had married Alice, daughter of Sir Walter de Windsor,[1] of Windsor in Devon, and he left three sons; the eldest, another Sir Richard, with whom we are not concerned, and two others both of whom were called Sir John. In the case of the first[2] of the two Sir Johns, there was this singular coincidence that while he had a brother of his own name, he married Alice Montgomery, who' had a sister of her own name. Genealogists would learn with relief that they died without issue.

The younger Sir John, who was Sir Adrian's father, died on July 28, 1500. His wife, Sir Adrian's mother, was Alice, the daughter of Sir Geoffrey Boleyn, Lord Mayor of London; and thus Sir Thomas Boleyn, whom Henry the Eighth made Earl of Wiltshire, became his brother-in-law, and consequently Anne Boleyn and Sir Adrian the Martyr were first cousins. Sir John, who was an Esquire of the Body to King Edward the Fourth, was sent by him as Sheriff into Cornwall, where he had to conduct the siege of St. Michael's Mount, which was defended by the Earl of Oxford. This was in 1471; in 1481 he was Sheriff of Hertfordshire and Essex, and in a year or two the King made him "Master Porter" of Calais. King Richard] the Third, who had succeeded by the murder of his nephew, sent Sir John Fortescue a fresh appointment as Esquire of the Body to the King, with a salary of fifty marks, which appointment carried with it the title of "Sir;" but Sir John Fortescue joined his old adversary the Earl of Oxford, and they offered their services to the Earl of Richmond, who soon after became Henry the Seventh. Landing at Milford Haven on August 6, 1485, on the 22nd the decisive battle of Bosworth Field was fought, in which Sir John, who had been knighted by Henry on his landing, took his part. The victory gave the throne without a rival to Henry the Seventh, and the King rewarded Sir John by making him, within a month of the battle, Chief Butler of England, and by many grants of forfeited manors. At the coronation he was made Knight banneret. Sir John was much at Court henceforward, among other occasions at the festivities in 1494, when Prince Henry, afterwards Henry the Eighth, then but two years old, was created Duke of York and a Knight of

---

[1] Sir Adrian Fortescue, July 26, 1533, gave 6s. 8d. "to the midwife and nurse at the christening of Walter, son to Sir Will. Wyndsore, besides a little gilt flagon weighing ½oz. [?] that I gave to my said godson." This godson will have been a cousin of his.

[2] The pedigree given by Lord Clermont at p. 234 in error calls him the younger.

the Bath. At length, crossing over to Calais with the King and Queen, in May, 1500, to avoid the plague, of which thirty thousand persons died in London in that year, his own life came to a close immediately after a speedy return to England, for he died at Punsborne July 28, 1500.

And now we come to our Sir Adrian. It is disappointing when trying to trace a history that ended with a glorious martyrdom, to have such very slight indications of the interior and spiritual life that preceded it. So it is in our case, but we must be thankful to emerge from black ignorance to the knowledge of such detail as Lord Clermont's diligent research has been able to collect for us respecting the martyr. The antiquarian gets more than the martyr's client, but the latter is not left without some comforting scraps.

Sir Adrian was born about the year 1476. He is first mentioned in 1499, when he was already married to Anne Stonor, daughter of Sir William Stonor of Stonor, near Henley-upon-Thames. The two families were doubly connected, for in 1495 his wife's brother, John Stonor, married his sister, Mary Fortescue. On the death of her brother John, Lady Fortescue inherited Stonor, but her right to it was disputed by her uncle Sir Thomas, and after his death, by her cousin Sir Walter. Stonor Park was, however, retained by Sir Adrian Fortescue till Michaelmas, 1534. Leland describes it as "a fair park, and a warren of conies, and fair woods. The mansion house standeth climbing on a hill, and hath two courts builded with timber, brick, and flint." The fair woods and park are there still, to speak for themselves and, better still, the ancient domestic chapel remains, dating from the year 1349, and it, like the equally ancient chapel of the Eystons at East Hendred in the adjoining county, has never been used for Protestant service. The old walls at Stonor speak to us, not only of the Venerable Adrian Fortescue, but also of the Blessed Father Campion, whose *Decem rationes* was printed at Dame Cecilia Stonor's park near Henley, and who himself stayed there to see his book through the press. Blessed Edmund could hardly have failed to know that a martyr had lived there before him.

To return to earlier days. In 1503, when Prince Henry, a boy of twelve, was created Prince of Wales and Earl of Chester, on the 18th of February, Sir Adrian was created a Knight of the Bath. Prince Arthur's marriage to Princess Catherine of Spain had been celebrated on November 14, 1501, and his death followed on the 2nd of April.   That marriage, so eventful in its consequences, and the other Royal marriage of the King's daughter Margaret to the King of Scotland, which conveyed to the Stuarts the right of succession to the Crown of England, were both officially brought before Sir Adrian Fortescue, as he was one of the Royal Commissioners for levying, from his county of Oxford, aids on those occasions to Henry the Seventh.   In 1511 he was put in the Commission of the Peace for the county, his name being the first named in the Commission.

Sir Adrian and his elder brother John of Herts—it is curious that the names, when mentioned conjointly, come in this order— are named together in bonds to pay various sums to the King as fines for murder, riot, &c., between 1503, in Henry the Seventh's time, and 1511, when Henry the Eighth was King. This does not mean that they were personally guilty of these offences, but that the fines were laid on their estates when the malefactors could not be found.   In 1512 the two brothers were amongst those who agreed to send a certain number of men for war service abroad, and accordingly, in the following year, they took part with the young King, Henry the Eighth, in his expedition into France.   At that time the King of England was in league with his wife's father, Ferdinand King of Aragon, with the Emperor Maximilian and with Pope Leo X., and the object of his invasion of France was to create a diversion in favour of Italy and the Papal States by attacking Louis the Twelfth in Flanders.   The King crossed the sea with twenty-five thousand men, of whom fourteen thousand formed "the King's ward" or division.   The Fortescues had received their orders on May 18, 1513, to be shipped, each of them with fifty archers and fifty bills, from Dover or Sandwich in the "middle ward," but they were afterwards transferred to the King's Ward.[3]   The ship in which they crossed was "the Mawdelen of Pole," or in modern spelling, the Magdalen of Poole, of one hundred and twenty tons, with eighty-seven men ; Sir Adrian Fortescue is called "captain," and the charge for the use of the ship for the month was 31*l.* 15*s.* 4*d.*   The Standards borne by the brothers are given in a manuscript in the College of Arms.   It will be

---

[3] "Ward" is of course the same word as "guard," and we still speak of the advance guard and the rear guard.   The latter word in the old spelling, "rereward," in the Protestant Bible, has puzzled many a reader.   It has sometimes been pronounced, "And I will be thy re-reward."

enough to give the bearings of one of Sir Adrian's banners, on which of course the crescent appears, to mark that he was the second son. "*Vert*, a heraldic tiger passant *argent*, maned and tufted *or*, charged on the shoulders with a crescent *sable*, between (in the dexter base and sinister chief) two antique shields *argent*, each charged with the word ffort, and three mullets also *argent*, charged with the crescent as before." Sir Adrian's motto was *Loyalle Pensée*, his brother's *Je pense loyalement.* The proper coat of the Fortescues—I omit the quarterings and escutcheon of pretence—was *Azure*, on a bend engrailed *argent*, cottised *or.*

The brothers will have been witnesses of the sights of this brief campaign. The first and most memorable sight was the Emperor Maximilian, "wearing a cross of St. George," and serving under the orders of the King of England. Some great military sights there were to see. On August 16, 1513, the French were struck by panic at the Battle of the Spurs, so called, says Holinshed, "forasmuch as they instead of sword and lance used their spurs, with all might and main to prick forth their horses to get out of danger." Another was the sad sight of the burning of Therouenne ; and a sight of another sort was the tournament held by King Henry, in the presence of Margaret Duchess of Savoy, in Tournay, when he had taken it. The Chronicle of Calais tells us that Sir Adrian Fortescue landed at Calais for this campaign on the 21st of June, and Sir John with the King on the last day of the month. They re-entered Calais on the 19th of October, and returned forthwith to England.

Sir John Fortescue was at a royal banquet at Greenwich just a month before his death in 1517. Sir Adrian was there too, and as both were present in a menial capacity, it may be as well to describe their positions. The banquet was held on St. Thomas's day ; that is to say, the summer feast, the 7th of July. There were in all thirty-three people seated at the banquet. The King had the centre place at the upper table, Queen Catherine was on his right, and Cardinal Wolsey on hers ; on the King's left was the French Queen, and the Emperor's Ambassador was beside her. Then at the side tables, with English peers and peeresses sat the Ambassadors of France, Arragon, and Venice.

To attend on these thirty-three persons no less than 250 names are given in a paper that was drawn up beforehand, and these are almost all lords or knights. How they could avoid being in one another's way is the difficulty. For instance: Lords Abergavenny, Fitzwalter, Willoughby, and Ferrers, to hold torches while the King washes. To bear towels and basons: for the King, the Earl of Surrey; Lords Richard Grey, Leonard Grey, and Clinton, Sir Maurice Berkeley, and eight other knights. The King's server was Sir William Kingston; and to attend on him, Lord Edmund Howard and fourteen knights, the last named of whom is Sir Adrian Fortescue. Amongst the directions we find: "All the gentlemen to be ready to serve the lords and ladies with drink." Sir Adrian was a Gentleman of the King's Privy Chamber, but the date of his appointment is not known.

In the following year, 1518, Sir Adrian lost his first wife. The exact date we learn from his own book of accounts, in which fortunately he unconsciously tells us much that concerns him. "Costes of the beryyng and [what was] done after for the Lady Anne Fortescue, which dyyd the xiiijth day of June A^o. D^i. 1518, & A^o. R[egni] R[egis] H[enrici] 8$^{vi.}$ 10, then Monday at Stonor." She was buried at Pyrton Church, close to Shirburn, and in the account we can trace the progress of the funeral, and see most of what was done. The knight begins his record with the purchase of his mourning: "for me and my daughter"—he had two daughters, but one of them was probably married. Then come the "lyvereys,"[4] for making up which he had 2lbs. of thread and needles, for which he paid 20d. Five women servants are named, in the inverse order of their importance, judging by the money given to them, Janet Andrewe, Dame Lewen, Mary Tesdale, Catherine Blackhall, and Margaret Robinson. After the people, we have four yards of black cotton for the pillions, the same for saddles, the same for the hearse, six yards of broad cotton for the wall, and six yards of narrow cotton for the rails, and two ells of linen for the hearse cross, the making and sewing of which cost 4d. We now leave Stonor, with an offering to the priests there of 14d. As the payments to the clerk and tailors of Henley were heavy, and we have the entry, "bringing the church gear," probably Stonor chapel was hung with the black hangings that belonged to Henley. A still larger sum was paid "to the church of Henley for hanging the church stuff;" and then, "for the costs of the Dirige and Mass there 8s. *Item*, to the stone, for the hearse light, that is, for the workings, 14s. 4d., and for the waste,

---

[4] There can be no object in continuing to give the old spelling.

9½ *lbs.*, 6s. 4d., and for four tapers of 6 *lbs.* weight, 4s. These the priest had as a duty to the vicar." So it seems that he only paid for what was consumed of the wax burnt round the coffin, but that the four altar candles of six pounds' weight—fine noble tapers, so called from their tapering form—went to the vicar. The wax was 2d. a pound, which, if we multiply by ten, to bring us the modern value, would be not far below our modern price.

Other things were not at all modern. Sir Adrian gave in "alms dole to beggars a penny a piece to 646 persons;" and his gift "to the preacher of the sermon" at Pyrton, was 10s., or in modern money, 5l. "To a priest singing there half a year, 46s. 8d., to the clerk of the church there, 3s. 4d., and for wine and wax, 10d."

The good Knight then summed up both sides, and it came to 38l. 7s. 4d., but there were plenty of other expenses afterwards to enter. The bellringers at the burying got 2s. 2d., the clerk of Shirburn 4d., twenty-four torchbearers, who came apparently from Shirburn to the funeral, 4s., to the parish priest there 12d. But there was a Dirige and Mass at Watlington, and payments for the waste of torches from Watlington, Henley, Shirburn, and Cupham. There were six ringers at Watlington : how many bells are there now? For the stone in the chancel the Vicar's deputy received 6s. 8d. But the great entry is, "To the priests (42), and clerks (4), and children (12) to serve and help Mass 23s. 4d., for wine and wax 2s., for Mass pence there 20d." What were these last? Not, it would seem, fees to the servers; but perhaps a silver penny given at the Offertory of each Low Mass.

The dinner at the burying cost no less than 10l. 13s. 6d. There were two beeves and nine muttons, seven lambs, four calves, ten geese, two capons, twenty-four couple of conies, and fifteen pigs. The cream, butter, eggs, salt and coals cost 7s. 1d. They sent over from Stonor twenty gallons of wine, eight kilderkins of beer, and a quarter of wheat in bread; but they had to get more than as much again of ale from Watlington, and more than six times as much bread. The last item of the dinner expenses is 3s. 8d. "to the barber of Watlington for his labour," though what he had to do with the dinner is not said. Besides the 646 poor people who received the penny dole, Sir Adrian notes that there were other poor persons there "by estimation 300 and above." A great funeral was an event for the neighbourhood, if nearly a thousand poor were benefited by it. The whole expense was 42*l.* 9*s.* 1*d.*, or in modern money say 425*l.*

Our readers may think that Sir Adrian had done enough, but he did not think so. Next comes the month's mind, and after that the year's mind. The first item for the month's mind is that "the Vicar's deputy had an ambling nag for the mortuary after the month's mind delivered." The month's mind was kept in three places : first his wife's burying-place at Pyrton, the Vicar of which parish received 2*s.*, forty-six priests there 24*s.*, the clerks and Mass helpers 7*s.* 2*d.* Benet for dressing altars 8*d.* The bellringers there 12*d.*, the Mass pence amounted to 3*s.* 8*d.*, that is forty-four pence, which nearly corresponds with the number of the priests ; so that, probably, that number of Masses were said that day on the temporary altars dressed by Benet, and the alms for each Low Mass seems to have been 6*d.*, which is just our 5*s.* At Stonor chapel there were six priests who received 4*s.*, a double alms probably in their case ; the Mass pence came to 6*d.*, again a penny for each Mass ; and the clerk and poor folk there had 6*d.* Then Sir Adrian adds, "*Item*, at the Savoy, I being there at London, in all fifteen Masses that day 5*s.*," which would be a lower alms of 4*d.* There was another great dinner at Pyrton, costing about half what the funeral dinner cost. There was a bullock to eat, and ten sheep, two calves, ten pigs, and ten geese. Eleven kilderkins of beer from Stonor, and twenty-one dozen of bread from Watlington, were sufficient this time. The butter to baste the meat cost 8*d.*, and three cooks were content with 2*s.* The forty-six priests, no doubt, had the places of honour at the table, but there must have been plenty to spare for the poor. The last item after the dinner accounts is 2*s.* for "singing, wine and wax." The comma is probably a mistake. The forty-six priests will have done the singing at the Requiem, and as altarbreads were commonly called "singing breads" till far into Elizabeth's reign, so probably the wine used at the altar is here called "singing wine."

The first year's mind at Pyrton has but one entry, besides its cost of 26*s.* 8*d.* in one sum. "*Item*, for 36 escutcheons of arms both in (12) metal and (24) colours, great and large, to give to divers churches in the country 36*s.*" He gave Pyrton Church a vestment of black velvet with the appurtenances, but he does not say what it cost. Pyrton was not intended by the good knight to be his wife's final resting-place. Bisham Priory on the Thames was the place chosen by him, and he set to work to raise a tomb to mark her grave. He gives his orders from monuments that he knew and admired, selecting them from the cloister of the Black Friars in London. To the Black Friars, the Order of St. Dominic, we may gather from a notice fifteen years later, he had a special devotion, for in the summer of 1534 he records, " Given to the Black Friar of Oxford to be in the Fraternity 12*d.*"⁵ In their London cloister he chose Sir Robert Southwell's tomb of marble, and had its like delivered to him in London by the marblers of Corfe in Purbeck, for 8*l.* This was the year after his wife's death. He had it taken to the Black Friars, and there he left it for some time, for he paid " the marbler of the Black Friars for the tomb lying with him two years 3*s.* 4*d.*" He paid 12*d.* " for the carriage of the said tomb to Paul's churchyard to the marbler there," and 66*s.* 8*d.* " to a marbler in Paul's churchyard for the pictures, writings, and arms, gilt after the rate of Sir Thomas of Parre's tomb in the Black Friars." The tomb was carried by water to Bisham, at a cost of 7*s.* 6*d.*, and the expense of its erection was 18*s.* 4*d.*

On the last day of March, 1525, nearly seven years after her death, Sir Adrian transferred his wife's body to Bisham Priory. A new coffin was made, and a horse litter to carry it, 26 yards of black cotton covered the litter and the horse, and an ell of linen cloth made the cross. Six escutcheons of arms were made, four of which were for Bisham. There were twelve staff torches of wax, and six torch-bearers all the way : five priests went with the body, and the clerk of Pyrton carried the cross the whole journey, which cross as well as the pall belonged to Henley. Seven priests received the body by the way at the three resting places, Tyfeld, Marlow, and Bisham parish church. The *cortège* had had " bread and drink at Pyrton Church first," and at Tyfeld Vicarage they dined. It was an abstinence day, and they had " 4 salt fishes 20*d.*, a ling 12*d.*, stock fishes 10*d.*, one salt salmon 14*d.*, four salt eels [congers] 16*d.*, fifty white herrings 12*d.*, forty red herrings 8*d.*, fresh fish 4*s.*" The mustard, salt, and onions cost 4*d.*, and the onions are written and no doubt called " ungeons." Three kilderkins of beer, eight casts of manchettes [the best kind of white bread], and twenty-six casts of household bread made up the meal, and when it was

⁵ This is taken, as some other extracts further on will be, from an account-book of Sir Adrian's in the Record Office, which has escaped Lord Clermont's notice. *Calendar, Henry VIII.* vol. 7, n. 243.

over, the knight paid 8*d.* "for making clean the Vicarage at Tyfeld and y⁰ wessel" [*la vaisselle*, the dishes and spoons].

Master Prior at Bisham was paid 66*s.* 8*d.* "for her laystone there," and 31*s.* 8*d.* was "given to him and his convent for the Dirige, the Mass, and other business." "The Vicar of Bisham for the claim of a mortuary," the funeral not being in his church, received 6*s.* 8*d.* Half that sum was paid to each of the churches at Pyrton, Tyfeld, and Marlow, and 2*s.* to Bisham parish church for torchwastes and ringings. The bread and drink at Bisham Priory at the burial cost 3*s.* 4*d.*, the torchbearers got 4*d.* for "drinking homeward," the men of Henley 14*d.* for drinking at Henley, "Master Whitton and the priests drinking at Marlow," 2*s.*

At Bisham, Lady Fortescue rested among her ancestors, Lord Clermont tells us, the Montacutes Earls of Salisbury, Richard Neville the King-maker, her grandfather's brother and her grandfather himself, the Marquis of Montague. But alas! she was not destined to rest there in peace. In August, 1538, Sir Adrian records that he has paid for his tomb again "at the rasing of Bisham Priory, 20*s.*" He had to repurchase it, for the King had given Bisham away bodily with all that it contained. So Sir Adrian had to pay for the taking it down and for the costs to the water, and for carrying it to Henley, "and for the image of the Trinity 8*d.*, and for a new small coffin 4*d.* Twenty years have gone by since her death, and all that remains of the wife of his bosom can now go into "a new small coffin ;" and he pays Richard Hall "for his labour in the said cause and bringing the coffin with the bones to Brightwell Church, and to the clerk for making the grave by the high altar there the 11th day of August." Sir Adrian Fortescue of Brightwell, Oxon, is what our martyr was called in the Act of Parliament that attainted him.

But we must not move on so fast. Before leaving funerals we must add that Sir Adrian bought "at the rasing of Abingdon monastery church" a high marble tomb, apparently for his own resting place some day ; but that, as we shall see, was not to be. And he erected a monument to his father at Bishop's Hatfield to which his brother contributed a small sum, and this shows that Sir Adrian, though the younger brother, was the wealthier of the two. He at the same time contributed largely to Hatfield Church, giving two great candlesticks for the altar, two "papis of bone and glass" (whatever they may be), two tin cruets, a

table of the crucifix, a table of the "Oracion," a vestment of
red camlet, two great forms and then four great forms more,
two towels for the priests' hands, a new great door (the wood
and iron work cost 40s., the lock 3s. 4d.), "a great tabernacle
for the altar, bought at Calais in the war time" for 20s., which
came to London by ship and then was sent down to Hatfield,
mended and set up, for 21s. 4d. more : at Michaelmas, 1526,
"a new altar cloth and two curtains of red and green French
say [serge], lined with buckram and fringed, price in all 11s.,"
3½ yards of blue buckram to cover the altar, 17½d.; and
lastly, "sent thither at Whitsuntide, 1529, two linen altar cloths
and a linen corporal after the robbing of the church," 7s. 6d.
Sir Humphrey, the priest, twice came up from Hatfield to see
Sir Adrian ; the costs of his journey the first time being 3s. 4d.
and the second time 20d.

We have now done with funerals, and we go back again to
the gay world, and indeed to the world at its gayest, for early
in 1520, Sir Adrian received a summons[6] from the King to
accompany the Queen to the Field of the Cloth of Gold. He
was bidden to take with him "ten tall personages well and
conveniently apparelled," and he was to appoint himself in
apparel as to his degree, the honour of the King and of the
realm, appertained ; but he was to convey with him over the
sea for his own riding and otherwise not above three horses, and
he was to repair to the Queen by the 1st of May.

On obeying this mandate, Sir Adrian must have seen
the landing of the youthful Emperor, who had been elected
to the Empire the year before. On Saturday, May 26,
1520, Charles the Fifth "arrived with all his navy of ships
royal on the coast of Kent, direct to the port of Hythe
the said day by noon, where he was saluted by the Vice-
Admiral of England, Sir William Fitzwilliam, with six of the
King's great ships well furnished, which lay for the safeguard
of passage betwixt Calais and Dover. Towards evening the
Emperor departed from his ships, and entered into his boat,
and coming to the land, was met and received of the Lord
Cardinal of York with such reverence as to so noble a prince
appertained. Thus landed the Emperor Charles the Fifth at
Dover, under his cloth of estate of the black eagle, all spread

---

6 Cotton. MSS. *Caligula*, D. vii. art. 118. It must be owing to the seizure of
Sir Adrian's property at his attainder that so many documents belonging to him are
found in the British Museum and the Public Record Office.

on rich cloth of gold.   He had with him many noble men and
many fair ladies of his blood.   When he was come on land, the
Lord Cardinal conducted him to the Castle of Dover, which
was prepared for him in most royal manner.   In the morning
the King rode with all haste to the Castle of Dover to welcome
the Emperor, and entering into the Castle alighted. . . . On Whit-
Sunday, early in the morning, they took their horses and rode to
the city of Canterbury, the more to keep solemn the feast of
Pentecost ; but specially to see the Queen of England, his aunt,
was the Emperor's intent, of whom ye may be sure he was most
joyfully received and welcomed. . . . The Emperor remained in
Canterbury till the Thursday, being the last of May, and then
taking leave of the King and of his aunt, the Queen, departed
to Sandwich, where he took his ships and sailed into Flanders.
The same day the King made sail from the port of Dover, and
landed at Calais about eleven of the clock, and with him the
Queen and ladies, and many nobles of the realm. . . . The 4th
of June the King and Queen with all their train removed from
Calais to his princely lodging newly erected beside the town of
Guisnes, the most noble and royal lodging that ever before was
seen."   And here we may leave Holinshed,[7] our good chronicler,
or else we shall have to follow him for many a page through all
the glories of the Field of the Cloth of Gold.   With those
splendours we have no need to trouble ourselves, except to
notice how completely the nobles and the knighthood and
gentlefolk of the country were at the King's command, and
how freely they could be called upon to spend their money.
It must have cost Sir Adrian not a little to apparel himself and
his "ten tall personages," so as to be in keeping with the reck-
less expenditure of Henry the Eighth and Francis the First.
At the same time it was an honour to be chosen on such an
occasion, of which no doubt many a knight would be jealous,
and the choice was in all probability a mark of favour on the
part of Cardinal Wolsey, by whom all the arrangements were
made.

Whether Sir Adrian accompanied King Henry to Gravelines
on the 10th of July, where the English King had an interview
with the Emperor, we do not know.   As he was in the Queen's
train it is more likely that he remained with her at Calais, but
the King and the Emperor came there on the next day, "and
there continued in great joy and solace, with feasting, banquet-

ing, dancing and masking until the 14th of July." Sir Adrian will have been one of the English lords and gentlemen who were "displaced of their lodgings" to entertain the suite of Charles. Before the end of the month our good knight was back again in England, and probably at home.

Two years later,[8] that is in 1522, when the King was expecting another visit from the Emperor, another summons came to Sir Adrian, "forasmuch as it is requisite he shall be honourably accompanied at that time with our lords and nobles both spiritual and temporal, as well for his cheerful and princely receiving, as to conduct him from place to place for the fame and renown of the realm." The King was then at his manor of New Hall in Essex, "otherwise called Beaulieu," as Holinshed says, "where the King had lately builded a costly mansion." The summons is dated the 4th of April, and Sir Adrian was required to be at Canterbury on the 27th of the same month ; but counter-orders came, and Sir Adrian was wanted for fighting and not for pageantry. On his summons he has written the memorandum. "After the preparation herefore, I was commanded to go to the sea under my Lord Admiral, where we were and on land twenty-one weeks."

We have a glimpse of Sir Adrian's preparation on a similar occasion in the following year, in a letter addressed to him in London by John Haywood,[9] who sends him a list of men, partly his tenants, who were mustered for July 1, 1523, with the armour to which they were admitted. One of the men, Thomas Hicks, Fortescue's farmer of Stynchecombe, Haywood could not find. He advises Sir Adrian to allow some to "buy their peace to bide at home, for ye may have prettier men in Henley than there." At Henley they were expecting him to call upon them, and are always ready.

The twenty-one weeks on sea and land, spent as Sir Adrian tells us with the Lord High Admiral, Thomas Howard, Earl of Surrey, were employed in part in "wafting the Emperor over to the coast of Biscay,"[10] in July, 1522, and then "finding the wind favourable, according to his instructions, the Admiral made to the coast of Brittany, and landing with his people, in number seven thousand, about five miles from Morlaix, marched thither,

---

[8] Lord Clermont has dated this letter two years too soon, not perceiving that Sir Adrian had himself endorsed it Anno xiiijto. that is to say 1522.

[9] Calendar, *Henry VIII.* vol. 3, n. 3148.

[10] Holinshed, vol. 3, p. 678.

and assaulting the town, won it. For the master gunner, Christopher Morris, having there certain falcons, with the shot of one of them, struck the lock of the wicket in the gate so that it flew open ; and then the same Christopher and other gentlemen with their soldiers, in the smoke of the guns pressed to the gates, and finding the wicket open entered, and so finally was the town of Morlaix won and put to the sack. The soldiers gained much by the pillage, for the town was exceeding rich, and specially of linen cloth. When they had rifled the town thoroughly, and taken their pleasure of all things therein, the Earl caused them by sound of trumpet to resort to their standards, and after they had set fire to the town and burned a great part thereof, the Earl retreated with his army towards his ships, burning the villages by the way, and all that night lay on land. On the morrow after, they took their ships, and when they were bestowed on board, the Earl commanded sixteen or seventeen ships, small and great, lying there in the haven to be burnt. . . . After this they continued awhile on the coast of Brittany, and disquieted the Bretons by entering their havens, and sometimes landing and doing divers displeasures to the inhabitants about the coast. After that the Earl had lain awhile thus on the coast of Brittany, he was countermanded by the King's letters, who thereupon brought back his whole fleet into a place called the Cow, under the Isle of Wight "—now-a-days we call it Cowes—" and then went on land himself, discharging the more part of his people, and leaving the residue with certain ships under the governance of the Vice-Admiral Sir William Fitzwilliam, to keep the seas against the French."

Even if Sir Adrian was then discharged, he was not able to go home, for on the 2nd of September of this same year, 1522, the Earl of Surrey with a powerful force—the Chronicle of Calais says fourteen thousand men—in which Sir Adrian Fortescue had his place, marched into Picardy, aided by "a great power of Burgognians," sent by the Regent of Flanders, Lady Margaret of Savoy. Of this expedition Holinshed says, "All the towns, villages, and castles in the country through which they marched were burned, wasted and destroyed on every side of their way." The Earl returned to Calais on the 16th of October, bringing " a marvellous great booty of goods out of the country," and he landed at Dover on the 24th of October. " All the residue of the army came over also with the navy, and arrived in the Thames ; and so every man into his country at his pleasure." And with this, Sir Adrian's twenty-one weeks of active service by sea and land came to an end. He must therefore have gone to sea in May.

We have already learnt that Sir Adrian was engaged in similar warfare on French soil in 1523, and John Haywood's letter has survived to tell us of his muster of his tenants for military service for the 1st of July.

On August 24, 1523, Charles Brandon, Duke of Suffolk, crossed over to Calais with an army which Wolsey said was the largest that had been sent out from England for a hundred years. Sir Adrian is mentioned by Holinshed as being in his train. The Castle of Bell was taken and rased to the ground at the end of September, the town of Braye was taken by assault on the 20th of October, Montdidier surrendered on the 27th. "The soldiers, being thus led from place to place, began to murmur among themselves and to grudge, because of the winter season, being nothing meet for their purpose to keep the fields : it grieved them that the Burgognians being provided of waggons, made shift to send the spoil and pillage home into their country, being at hand, and they to want such means to make the best of those things which they got, so that, as they took it, they beat the bush and others had the birds. This grudge was yet by gentle words ceased for a time. . . . After great rains and winds which had chanced in that season, there followed a sore frost, which was so extreme that many died for cold, and some lost fingers, some lost toes, so extreme was the rigour of that frost." The result of the "intemperate weather, the lack of victuals, and such other discommodities," was that the Duke of Suffolk, led back his army to Valenciennes, and so by Flanders to Calais, to the displeasure of the King who was preparing to send reinforcements under William Blount, Lord Mountjoy. When Sir Adrian got home we do not know, but this seems to be the end of his personal experience in the French wars. His tenants, however, had not done with them, for in a letter under the King's signet from Richmond, dated April 1, 1528, the King says that he has "determined to send a certain crew of men, well elect and chosen" for the defence of Guisnes under Lord Sandys, its captain ; to which crew Sir Adrian was ordered "to send the number of ten persons, footmen, archers, and other, to be well elect and tried," and these were to appear at Guildford on the 3rd of May, "sufficiently harnessed and appointed for the war," there to be viewed by Lord Sandys.

c

And now that we have done with the wars, we turn again to our scanty records of Sir Adrian's domestic life. By his first wife he had two daughters, Margaret who married Thomas Lord Wentworth, and Frances, the wife of Thomas Fitzgerald, Earl of Kildare. Thomas, tenth Earl of Kildare, "Silken Thomas" he was called from the silken fringe he and his body-guard wore on their helmets, had risen against the English Government in Ireland, and having given himself up to the Lord Deputy on August 18, 1535, was sent to the Tower and there imprisoned until February 8, 1537; when he was, with five of his uncles, hanged, drawn, and quartered at Tyburn. He was only twenty-four years old, so that it would seem that his wife must have been considerable older then he. During his imprisonment the long suit for the possession of Stonor was brought to an end by the Act of Parliament that confirmed the King's award. Stonor Park and one share of the estate was adjudged to Sir Walter Stonor, and the other share to Sir Adrian and to his two daughters after him. And as poor "Silken Thomas" was in the Tower, "a detestable and heinous rebel and traitor to the King's Highness," and so could not agree to the award, it was enacted that nevertheless the Lady Frances should have the benefit of it and that she and her husband should be bound by it. The suit between the two claimants of Stonor Park was not carried on merely in the King's Courts, for Sir Adrian was impoverished and his life disturbed by many "riots, assaults, and affrays" between his followers and those of his wife's cousin, Sir Walter. The contest was practically ended by the King's arbitration in 1534, the date of which is determined by two entries in his accounts, first of 10s. "to the King's Attorney's clerk for writing the King's award," and in Trinity Term 26 Henry VIII. (1534) 20s. 4d. "for the seal of the King's arbitrement between me and Sir Walter Stonor."

In a collection of proverbs made by our Sir Adrian, one is, "An old man is daft that marries a young woman." A man of fifty is not old, and so the proverb did not touch Sir Adrian himself, but the disproportion of age was considerable between him and his second wife, for at their marriage he was twice as old as she was, and half as much again. This was about the year 1530, she being twenty years old and he at east fifty. His first wife had been dead about twelve years when he married another Anne, this time the daughter of Sir William Rede, of Boarstall, Bucks.

Little presents to his mother-in-law from time to time figure comically in his accounts. "For two pair of knit sleeves to give to my Lady Rede 2*s.* 6*d. Item*, paid for 40 oranges for my Lady Rede 4*d. Item*, paid for six gallons and a pottle of sack 5*s.* 5*d.* a firkin 8*d. Item*, paid for an ell and ½ of canvas to truss it in 6*d.*, sent to my Lady Rede of gifts." The accounts seem to show that his wife's brother Austin and her sisters Bridget and Margaret, became members of his family, for there are homely entries of linen for Austin's shirts and buckram (save the mark) for Margaret's smocks; and while he was in prison he paid for a yard of yellow Briges [Bruges] satin for Margaret and Bridget's sleeves. Indeed Austin Rede was otherwise called Austin Fortescue. He must have gone to Winchester, for three books were sent there to him, and Sir Adrian makes a payment in July 1533 to the Warden of New College at Winchester 33*s.* 4*d.*

Sir Adrian's second wife bore him three sons, John, who became Queen Elizabeth's Privy Councillor, Thomas and Anthony, and two daughters Mary and Elizabeth. The birth of his second son is entered thus in his manuscript book, now in the Bodleian :

Thomas Fortescue, second son to Sir Adrian Fortescue knight, was born at Shirburn in the county of Oxford the Wednesday, being the 13th day of May in the 26th year of King Henry the Eighth, Anno Dñi 1534, *hora secunda post meridiem.* Godfathers at the Baptism were Thomas Rede, Thomas Whitton ; Godmother the Lady Williams ; God-father at the Confirmation the Bishop of Oxon, that was Abbot of Thame.

The latter portion, at all events, of this entry was not written by Sir Adrian, for his martyrdom was in 1539, and the see of Oxford was not erected by Henry the Eighth before 1541, when Robert King, the last Abbot of Osney, was appointed to it. Confirmation followed in those days at once upon Baptism, and the list of Sponsors in Henry the Eighth's time always concludes with the Godfather or Godmother, according to the sex of the child, "at the bishopping."

The children figure very curiously in the accounts. In the March and April before the birth of the second son, Sir Adrian gave "to Richard Ford's wife at my seeing my young son 4*s.* 8*d.* Given to Ford's wife the 8th day of April in reward [that is, as a gift] at Shirburn 3s. 8d.   For a girdle for Ford's wife 20d.   For an apron of worsted, wrought with gold, for Ford's wife, given her by my wife 2s. 6d." It would seem as though the eldest boy had been sent out to nurse, as undoubtedly the younger children were for a time when Stonor was handed over to Sir Walter, for we have then in the margin of the account-book "children's board" to these entries. "Paid for a month to Thomas Fortescue his norise [*nourrice*, nurse], beginning the 4th day of September 2s. 8d.   *Item*, paid for a month for Mary Fortescue to W. Thomas, begining the 10th day of September 3s. 4d.   *Item*, paid for Thomas Fortescue's nursing for two months, ending the 27th day of November 5s. 8d.   *Item*, paid to W. Thomas's wife, for Mary Fortescue her board, one month ending at Hallow-tide 3s. 4d.   *Item*, given to her when she carried her to my Lady Rede the — day of October and there delivered her 20d." We have other homely entries about the children.   "For two pair of schone [shoes] to my daughter Mary 4d.   A bonnet for John Fortescue, bought at Reading Fair 8d.   A bonnet for Thomas Fortescue 2s. 8d.   For two night bonnets for Thomas my son 10d."

We are now close upon the time of what Sir Adrian calls his "trobilles," the troubles that came upon him through the King's proceedings in religion.   Certainly it would not appear that Sir Adrian precipitated matters.   His name appears amongst those to whom lands were assigned out of Wolsey's possessions on his disgrace in July, 1530, and this does not seem like being in the King's bad books.   On the occasion of the Coronation of Anne Boleyn, who it will be remembered was Sir Adrian's first cousin, his name occurs [11] more than once.   He is among the knights and gentlemen appointed to be servitors "to attend upon the Queen's grace, the Bishop and the ladies sitting at the Queen's board in the Great Hall at Westminster;" and later on, in the same document, he is appointed one of the servitors to the Archbishop, Thomas Cranmer to wit.   Still more marked is the entry in his accounts [12] of 3s. 4d. "to the King's messenger on the 20th of September, 1533, for bringing the Queen's letter of the Princess Grace's birth, dated at Greenwich, the 7th"— the Princess Grace, who was born at Greenwich on that day, being the future Queen Elizabeth.   Surely Anne Boleyn did not

[11] *Calendar, Henry VIII.* vol. 6, n. 562.   Anne Boleyn was crowned June 1, 1533.   Cranmer had been consecrated on the 30th of March.
[12] *Calendar, Henry VIII.* vol. 7, n. 243.

send her letters by King's messengers on such an occasion to many knights of Sir Adrian's position. It seems plain that though he must have known full well that his cousin's marriage with a man whose wife was alive was no marriage, he thought it no business of his, in the words [13] of Sir Thomas More, "to murmur at it or dispute upon it." Besides, it must be remembered that sentence was not given by the Pope, declaring Queen Catherine's marriage valid, till March 23, 1534. There is no other indication of vacillation on Sir Adrian's part—not even the purchase for 10*d.* of the *Plowman's Tale* and *Colyn Clowte*, [14] nor the fancy for the *Plowman's Tale* that made him transcribe the greater part of it. A man may buy and read books that all the world is talking of, and yet not agree with all that he reads. Sir Adrian bought other books too, but not very many. He gave 3*d.* "for two prognostications, [15] and a book of algryrn" [arithmetic] ; "for five small English books 9*d.*; for a large matins book for myself 16*d.*" "*Item*, for two psalters 18*d.*, and for ink ½*d.*" "The book of the Acts of Parliament anno 25°" cost him 10*d.* Another time the entry is "for filling the ink bottle 4*d.*; for ten quires of fine paper, ½ a ream 6*d.*"

We have seen that Sir Adrian was admitted into the fraternity of the Black Friars at Oxford in July, 1533. He had previously taken a still more important step than this, for in 1532 he was admitted a Knight of St. John of Jerusalem. That distinguished military Order had been driven from Rhodes in 1522, and had acquired the island of Malta from the Emperor in 1530. Sir Adrian will have been received by Sir William Weston, at that time Lord Prior of the Knights of St. John, whose heart was broken, eight years after Sir Adrian joined the Order, by its destruction in England and the confiscation of its possessions. [16] As Sir Adrian was a married man, he

---

[13] *Calendar, Henry VIII.* vol. 7. n. 289.

[14] "Hereafter followeth a little book called *Colyn Clout*, compiled by Master [John] Skelton, Poet Laureate," London. In 8vo, without date. Skelton died in 1529.

[15] Nothing apparently but a kind of barometer. "Prognostications" appear more than once in the Privy Purse Expenses of Henry the Seventh, and among the effects of Henry the Eighth was a "Prognostication covered with green velvet" (*Excerpta Historica*, part i. p. 88).

[16] The Knights did not resign their goods into the King's hands, and they were suppressed by Act of Parliament. "Will. Weston, Knight, Prior of the Hospital of St. John of Jerusalem in England, during his life to have an annual rent of 1000*l.* and such reasonable portion of the goods and chattels of the said house as the King shall appoint him." This Parliament met on the 18th of April, 1540, and "on the 7th of May Sir Will. Weston, Knight, Lord Prior of St. John of Jerusalem without Smith-.

could only have been admitted as a Knight of Devotion ; unlike in this respect to his fellow-martyr, Sir Thomas Dingley, a Knight of Justice, preceptor of the commandery of Baddysley and Mayne at the time of the suppression.[17]

There is some further knowledge of Sir Adrian Fortescue's life during the interval before the storm burst, to be learned from this book of accounts. We begin with January, 1534, when he received from John Ford the rents of his lands in Devon. His bailiff accounts to him for the rents of his manors of Redyng and Beneschevys, Watcombe and Watlington, Stonor and Rushall. There is mention also of estates in Suffolk and Essex, for which his son-in-law, Lord Wentworth, paid him rent. He received 100 marks from the executors of the Archbishop of Canterbury, William Warham, who died August 23, 1532. He took his greyhounds from Stonor to Shirburn at the beginning of 1534. On the 23rd of January he rode to London, taking in his purse from Shirburn 22*l*. 6*s*. 8*d*. ; he stopped on the way at Colnbrook, and he took with him Master Chamberlayne, whose costs he paid. He probably found London in a fog, as his first payment was 6*d*. for a torch-link. His horses were sent home by Robin and Thome his servants. His first business in London was to lay in a stock of meagre food, which he calls "Lent stuff," on which he expended [18] 4*l*. 9*s*. 2*d*., and this he sent home by the Thames.

In London he stayed at "his lodgings," that is to say, a house in Blackfriars rented by him, the rent [19] paid for which

field, died, and never received any part of his pension ; and the King took all the lands that belonged to that house and that Order into his hands to the augmentation of his Crown, and gave [of] it to every of the challengers above written [at a Jousting at Westminster on May Day] for a reward of their valiantness 100 marks and a house to dwell in of yearly revenues out of the said lands for ever" (Stowe, *Chronicles*, pp. 579, 580). "*Cade*, a barrel of 500 herrings or of 1,000 sprats " (*Encyc. Dict.*).

[17] *Calendar, Henry VIII.* vol. 7. nn. 1138, 1675.

[18] "A barrel and half of white herrings 24*s*. A cade [*cadus*] of red herrings 7*s*. 3 cades of sprats 4*s*. 6*d*. 2 couple of beaten stock fishes 8*s*. 4*d*. 6 salmon 10*s*. 40 salt eels 14*s*. 4*d*. Half a barrel to put them in 6*d*. 2 baskets and cord 10*d*. An ell of canvas 4*d*. for the wharfage and water bailiff 4*d*. 2 ropes of great onions 10*d*. 100 oranges 10*d*., and for 24 sweet oranges 8*d*. For a piece of figs dodes (?) containing 30 *lbs*. 2*s*. 6*d*. 30 *lbs*. of raisins 2*s*. 6*d*. 10 *lbs*. of almonds 2*s*. 6*d*. 6 *lbs*. wine of sugar 2*s*. 3*d*. 6 *lbs*. of prunes 6*d*. A basket and line 4*d*. 2 hogsheads of claret 50*s*., and costs 8*d*." "*Cade*, a barrel of 500 herrings or of 1000 sprats " (*Encyc. Dict.*).

[19] His landlord was Richard Bishop, his tailor, who made his black gown and his riding coat for 2*s*. each, and who was useful to him in other ways, as he paid him for the carriage of his wood (making him a present of two loads of billets, besides his 14*s*. 8*d*.), and "for a Malmesey vessel and a pottle [2 quarts] to fill it 16*d*." Sir Adrian paid 6*s*. 5*d* "to the parson for the tithe of my house rent at London, after at the rate of] 11*d*. of the noble [6*s*. 8*d*.], of 10*l*. 16*s*. 8*d*. old rents, and due for one year at Easter anno xxv*to*. RR. Henr. viijti." [1533].

the Easter following was 16s. 8d. He was in London twenty
days, and amongst his payments we find 12d. "to the grooms in
the King's chamber," which seems to mean that he had an
audience of the King. He had law business in London, and
some of it seems to have been in the Ecclesiastical Court, for
in accordance with the custom of the age, he sends a present
to Cranmer's Chancellor, John Cox, LL.D.; and a curious
present it was: "for wyne and orange pyys [pies] sent to
Doctor Cokkes on Friday 2s. 4d. Sent thither on Saturday,
at night, Ipocras[20] [and] wafers 3s." He bought a bonnet of
velvet for his wife for 24s. and two yards of fine holland for
her "cresomes"—probably the chrisom cloth for her children's
christenings. Sir Adrian rode home taking with him his cousin
Lewis Fortescue, who was afterwards a Baron of the Exchequer,
whose law services he wanted for the coming Oxford Assizes, in
some suit of his against one Ambrose Pope. Among the
expenses of his stay at Oxford for the Assizes, now and again
later, he mentions "to the friars and crier 8d." What they had
to do with one another, that they should twice be linked
together, does not appear. It must not be overlooked that
our Knight, on the occasion of his visit to London, "gained
at play 7l. 3s. 3½d." which was a very considerable sum at that
period.

Then came another short journey to London for a few days
in the month of March; and on his return a journey into
Gloucestershire, with six servants, to purchase the manor of
Lasborow, near Tetbury, from William Nevyle, Esq., and to
take possession of that of Bradeston, which he had previously
bought. He started on Friday, the 20th of March, dined at
Abingdon and slept at Faringdon; the next day, Saturday,
he dined at Cyrsyter [Cirencester], stopped at Tetbury and
Lasborow, and slept at Bradeston, where his farmer and the
Warden of Bradeston entertained him. He reckoned that
it cost the farmer 10s. 9d. and the Warden 29s. 2d. He spent
Saturday night and all Sunday here, and Monday and Tuesday
he was at Lasborow. He there dined with Mr. Nicholas Wyke,
of whom he bought 1,500 sheep, and he gave 7s. to John
Boughton and William Cox of Burton who came to view
them. The next day was Lady Day, on which he heard

---

[20] *Hippocras*, a beverage composed of wine with spices and sugar, strained
through a cloth. It is said to have taken its name from "Hippocrates' sleeve," the
term apothecaries gave to a strainer (*Halliwell*).

Mass at Faringdon, and the 18*d.* he has entered for it was probably his offering at it. He dined that day at Abingdon and slept at Fairford "on our Lady Day at night." The next day home.

Poor man! When he got home he found Swallow, the King's messenger, waiting for him, bringing him Mr. Cromwell's letters to come to the King's Grace; and, paying the messenger 3*s.* 4*d.*, he started for London that day and remained there till the 30th of March, "Monday the morrow after Palm Sunday, that is five [days] in all on't, 28*s.*," which he enters as his "costs to and at London in Passion week." What he was summoned for we do not know, but the Parliament which had passed the Act of Succession was prorogued on the same 30th of March, "and there every lord, knight and burgess and all other were sworn to the Act of Succession and subscribed their hands to a parchment fixed to the same." [21] The oath was imposed by an Act passed on the very last day of the session. It was on the 13th of April that Blessed John Fisher and Blessed Thomas More refused to take the oath of succession, and went into the imprisonment from which death set them free more than a year later. It is not known that Sir Adrian was called upon to take the oath of succession, but he must have returned home with a lively consciousness of coming dangers. "During the Parliament time every Sunday at Paul's Cross preached a Bishop, declaring the Pope not to be supreme head of the Church." [22] The Act of Supremacy was not passed until the next Parliament which met in November, but there was quite enough in these sermons and in the Acts of Parliament of 1533–4 which he bought and took home with him, and especially in the terms of the oath of succession, to make him resolve to be prepared.

He came home by Assenden, staying at Hochtyde Court, and on his return to Shirburn, he gave presents "to the wives" of the neighbouring parishes, Salley, Pishull, Pirton and Shirburn "for the church." He also gave "to the bonfires, to drink, besides wood, 8*d.* To the wives to drink on St. Thomas's even at the fire 8*d.*" [23] Again his stay at home was very short,

[21] Holinshed, vol. 3, p. 792.

[22] Holinshed, vol. 3, p. 792.

[23] The eve of the Translation of St. Thomas, July 6, seems to have been thus kept. For instance, at Canterbury, in the accounts of the City Chamberlain, we have "1517-18. For 10*lbs.* of gunpowder against the watch on St. Thomas's even, *pretium libræ* 8*d.* 1521-2. For a staff and a banner to bear before the mayor's.

for on the 29th of April he started once more for London.   This time his business was the conclusion of his lawsuit with Sir Walter Stonor.   He was met on reaching London by two King's messengers, and he enters in his accounts the names of the lawyers [24] he employs and the fees he gives them "for devising answers to Sir Walter Stonor's articles."   His own plea was that "by the courtesy of England" he was entitled to his wife's property for his life and her children after him. He went to Greenwich, where the King probably was, on Ascension Day, again on the Friday, and on Sunday, the 10th of May, paying a couple of shillings boat hire each time. Among his various expenses we have the simple entry, "Paid for 4 pair of small shoon for my little son John and Mary 11*d.*" His costs in London were 4*l.* 8*s.* for himself and two servants, and he reached home once more on the 22nd of May.   During this absence his second son Thomas was born.

On the 9th of June he set out for London again and he returned on Sunday the 21st.   On the 3rd of July his face was turned towards London once more, and in the midst of this absence he paid 8*d.* "for carrying a letter to my wife in haste." His business in the Archbishop's Court must now have ended, for he enters, "Given to Mr. Chancellor Dr. Cox's servants to make merry 4*s.* 8*d.*   For writing the two acquittances and releases 2*s.*   Given to Mr. Dr. Cox's porter 4*d.*"   His return home this time was on the 11th of July.

After attending the Assizes at Oxford to carry on his suit against Ambrose Pope, he returned to Shirburn, and after the entry, "for laces for the maidens 4*d.*," he quietly records : "*Memorandum.*   Here I was committed to the Knight Marshal's ward at Woodstock," on the 29th of August, 1534. Vaughan, the groom of the King's chamber, came for him

pikes and the guns on St. Thomas's eve.   1527-8. For 9 *lbs.* of corn powder for the watch on St. Thomas's even (Dr. Brigstocke Sheppard's report; Hist. MSS. Commission, 9th rep. App. p. 152).   The First Vespers were always solemnly kept. Thus in 1504 the offerings at "the Martyrdom" in Canterbury Cathedral were, on the eve 7*s.*, and the feast of the Translation 3*s.* 4*d.* (*Ibid.* p. 126).   It was on the eve that Blessed Thomas More was martyred.   "To-morrow," he wrote to his daughter Margaret, "is St. Thomas of Canterbury's eve, and the Utas [octave day] of St.Peter ; and therefore to-morrow I long to go to God."

[24] Given to Mr. Brown and Mr. Chenley and Sir H. Wingfield 20*s.*, and to Bradshawe 10*s.*, and to Mr. Baldwyn 5*s.* for a drawing and devising of the answer to Sir Walter Stonor's articles, 35*s.*   Paid for writing the answer to the articles of Stonor 2*s.*   Paid for the copy of the same articles 20*d.*   Given to the Processar to stay all the actions 5*s.*

C *

to Shirburn, and got 5s. for his fee.   They started off by Watlington, and there they had to wait for the horses to be shod, which cost 18d.   Then on to Woodstock, where he paid for his servants' dinner and for "horsemeat"—in another place he called it "horsebread"—16d.   To appear before the authorities he had to change his riding dress, so he records, "Given for house room at Sygewykes [Sedgwick's] to shift me in, 12d."   He received orders to leave Woodstock, for his costs were 8s. "at Thame that Saturday at night," and 6s. 8d. he had to pay "to a man who was sent to fetch me again back to Woodstock and to Sir Thomas Wentworth's servant;" and so next comes a payment of 8d. this time "to Sygewyke's wife again for room at Woodstock," and then he is at Thame on Sunday at night, paying 9s.; and 16d. was "given to the priest to say Mass two days at my inn."   It is curious to see that Mass was said for Sir Adrian "at his inn," both at Woodstock and at Thame, for he was not two nights in any one place.   Was the prisoner not allowed to hear Mass in the church?   For prisoner he was, travelling in the custody of Richard Wentworth, the Knight Marshal's namesake and servant, as a gift to whom his wife here gave 20d.   Lady Fortescue will have come to Thame to meet him, anxious to know the result of the examination to which he was subjected at Woodstock, and doubly anxious on account of the delay caused by his recall there after he had once left it.   The payments at Thame are heavy because Lady Fortescue was there.   The gift to the officer in charge of him is in perfect keeping with the ways of the time; and it was always most galling to have to pay pursuivants and King's messengers when they were most unwelcome.

On Monday night he was at Uxbridge, and from the double cost 4s. it is plain that he paid his warder's expenses, as well as his own.   On Tuesday, the 1st of September, he went from Uxbridge to his lodging and Southwark by boat for 5d. and his "gear," that is his luggage cost 1d. more than himself.   That same day then, he was taken to the Marshalsea Prison, which was in Southwark.   When he got there he had to send out for sixpenny-worth of "trussing cord to truss his beds," and he bought ten faggots for 4d. and two *lbs.* of candles for 3d.   His dinner was at his lodging on Wednesday, and it cost him 12d., and "a quart of wine on Wednesday at dinner 2d."   The quart of wine seems to have lasted him for three days, if not four; for his next entry for his food is "wine on Saturday, at night, and pears and beer 6*d.* ; " and then he laid in something of a stock, "wine on Sunday and pears 16*d.*" and he gave the same sum to his man, Robin, who brought him venison and "a fardell," a parcel of provision for his wants, sent by the good wife at home. "Thome," his other man, stayed with him all the time of his imprisonment,—Thomas Honychirch was his name : and another man, John Hawcliff, came from Shirburn through "Wykm" (Wycombe) to London, but on the 13th of September he received his year's wages in full, "for he shall be shortly married," and he "went clearly from me on Wednesday, the 23rd," having been three weeks in the prison with his master. Sir Adrian paid the Knight Marshal 10*s.* a week for his own board, and 3*s.* 4*d.* a week for each of his men. On the 10th of September he had Mr. Whitton to sup with him, his second boy's godfather, the old friend who had accompanied him ten years before, when he carried his wife's body to Bisham. That supper cost him 2*s.* 7*d.*, and he spent 2*s.* "for wine and nuts on Sunday and Holy Rood day [Monday, the 14th] in all, with part thereof given to Mr. Prior at my two suppers with him." This was probably Robert Strowddyll, Prior of the Dominicans, with whom he will have been intimate in consequence of the nearness of his house in London to the Convent of the Black Friars.[25] Prior Strowddyll, alas, had signed the repudiation of the Pope and the acknowledgment of the King's Supremacy on the 17th of the preceding April.

Lady Fortescue was at Woodstock "at St. Matthew's-tide in September," where the Court was, and Dolphin brought his master letters, we may well suppose that they were from her, on Michaelmas Day. They were followed by herself on Thursday, the 1st of October, and 31*s.* 9½*d.* were her "costs with four servants and three horses at London from Thursday afternoon to Monday in the morning, in all, besides her baiting at Colnbrook the 5th day of October." It was an awkward time for the heads of the family to be absent from home, for Stonor was now being given up. Mr. Richard Crispe wrote "the

[25] Stowe says that the Dominican Friars "sometime had their house in Olde-borne [Holborn], where they remained for the space of fifty-five years, and then in the year 1276 Gregory Rocksley, mayor, and the Barons of this city, granted and gave to Robert Kilwarby, Archbishop of Canterbury, two lanes or ways next the street of Baynard's Castle and also the Tower of Mountfichet, to be destroyed ; in place of which the said Robert builded the late new Church of the Black Friars, and placed them therein" (*Survey of London*, 1603, p. 341).

Inventory indented of the deliverance of Stonor Place," divers persons were paid "to help to truss stuff at Stonor," the cattle were driven and marked at removing, and carts were hired for 28*s.* to carry his stuff and goods from Stonor at Michaelmas, "besides gift carts and mine own two carts." Lady Fortescue saw to it, but she wanted to be with her husband in prison, and so no wonder that her baby was put out to nurse and her little Mary sent to the care of her mother, Lady Rede.

On the 18th of October Sir Thomas Wentworth rode northward, the prisoner having been five weeks and two days in his custody. Accounts were settled between them and a new arrangement made. "Thenceforth I boarded myself and provided for all manner of necessaries for myself, my wife, my servants, and for all other *in the house there*, at my charge, as it appeareth in the household book there, entered and written, at the desire and request of the same Sir Thomas, and so continued during the time of my being in his ward and custody." Lord Clermont understands this to mean that Sir Adrian went to live in his own house, but if that had been so, the whole entry was needless. "The house there" was evidently the Marshalsea, and "the household book there" that kept by the Under-Marshal. At the time of this change Sir Adrian gave Richard Wentworth "a lion and a collar" that cost 12*d.*, and he contributed 8*d.* to Mrs. Under-Marshal to her servant's marriage offering. "*Item*, paid to Sir Thomas Wentworth's servants for going three times with me to my house 12*d.*"

His wife then came to live with him at the Marshalsea, and he bought "a low turned chair" for her. His servants, Richard Gregory and John Horsman had new tawny liveries that Michaelmas, and among many domestic entries, we have "a lye pot and two pictures of our Lady," and "a holy water stoup of pewter with the sprinkler," to give the place a Christian look. And there the sad year ran out. The kind-hearted old knight "lent to Harry, Sir Thomas Darcy his servant, to be repaid by his master or by him, to help him out of the King's Bench, in ward for a fray in Southwark, 7*s.* 6*d.*" And there are New Year's gifts. "A velvet bonnet for to give Mrs. Marshall, 11*s.*" and "a dozen gloves to give Mr. Marshall, 3*s.*"—more probably, it would seem, Mrs. Under-Marshal was the recipient ; and Mr. Mynton had 20*d.* and two young boys 8*d.*—New Year's gifts, be it noted, not Christmas boxes.

An entry respecting Lady Fortescue is significant. "For my wife's boat hire to Greenwich before Christmas, and three times in Christmas, and on Sunday after Christmas, 10*s.*" From which we gather that the Court was at Greenwich that Christmas, and that Lady Fortescue went there again and again to intercede for her husband.

The account-book now comes to an end, and I hope that my readers are as sorry as I am. The last entry is "paid for the Acts of this last Parliament 7*d.*," and a very bad seven pennyworth they were. The 3rd of November the Parliament began again," says Holinshed, "in the which was concluded the Act of Supremacy, which authorized the King's Highness to be Supreme Head of the Church of England, and the authority of the Pope abolished out of the realm." It would take a higher power than Parliament to do either the one or the other, and Sir Adrian Fortescue died for his faith in Him whose acts Parliament was not competent to repeal.

But the end was not quite yet. How long Sir Adrian continued in the custody of the Knight Marshal we do not know ; but the last date mentioned in his accounts is Shrove Sunday, or the Sunday before Lent [Feb. 7], 1535, when he paid Richard Hall for "his costs home." He will probably have been no longer a prisoner on the 4th of May, when Blessed Richard Reynolds, the three Carthusian priors, and John Hales were martyred at Tyburn, or on the 19th of June, when three other Blessed Carthusian martyrs were executed, and again on the 22nd of June and the 6th of July, when Blessed John Fisher and Blessed Thomas More were beheaded. Whether he was a prisoner in London or a free man at home, he knew what these events foreboded.

The year 1536 came, and on the 7th of January, Catherine of Arragon, the ill-used Queen of England, died. On the 19th of May Anne Boleyn was beheaded, and on the following day Henry married Jane Seymour.

Sir Adrian Fortescue possessed a Missal, which it is hoped yet exists [20] to be regarded as the relic of a Martyr. It was, of course, according to the Sarum rite, a book printed at Rouen in

[20] When Nichols was compiling his *History of Lancashire*, this missal was the property of the representative of Sir Adrian's family, Mr. Fortescue Turville, of Husbands Bosworth.

1510. In it he had entered his father's *obit*, and that of his first wife; and it bore the words, in his own handwriting, *Liber pertinet Adriano Fortescu militi*. This Missal serves to record Sir Adrian's opposition to the religious pretensions of King Henry the Eighth. It has inserted in it, "An order and form of bidding of beads by the King's commandment, anno 1536," the year after the deaths of our first Blessed Martyrs, the year of the deaths of Anne Boleyn and of her victim, Queen Catherine of Arragon, the year of Henry's marriage to Jane Seymour. Through the words that are printed here in italics Sir Adrian Fortescue drew his pen, an act that was high treason by King Henry's laws.

Ye shall pray for the whole congregation of Christ's Church, and especially for this Church of England.

Wherein I first commend *to your devout prayers the King's most excellent Majesty, Supreme Head immediately under God of the spirituality and temporality of the same* Church, and the most noble and virtuous Lady, Queen Jane, his most lawful wife.

Secondly, ye shall pray for the Clergy, and Lords temporal and Commons of this realm, beseeching Almighty God to give every one of them in his degree grace to use themselves in such wise as may be to His contentation, the King's honour, and the weal of the realm.

"Thirdly, ye shall pray for the souls that be departed, abiding the mercy of Almighty God, that it may please Him the rather at the contemplation of our prayers to grant them the fruition of His presence.

"God save the King."

All is now very nearly told. We have already seen that on March 14, 1538, he bought for 29*s.* 6*d.* a marble tomb and another great laystone at the pulling down of Abingdon Abbey Church," and he left it with William Wykes, "dwelling in Abingdon, at the sign of the White Hart." Perhaps he meant it for his own tomb, but his body was to receive no honour from men.

In February, 1539, he was arrested. On the 10th he wrote from London a letter to Henry Bourchier, Earl of Essex,[27] begging him earnestly to relieve him of a charge of 100*l.* due

---

[27] The Earl had long been on these terms with the Fortescues. "July 1, 1511, Henry Bourchier Earl of Essex and John Fortescue of Punsborne in the county of Hertford, Esquire [Sir Adrian's father], are bound by an obligation to pay 1,514*l.* within two months" (Henry VIII. accounts, Brit. Mus. Add. MSS. 21,480). "Henry Earl of Essex to Cromwell. Sir Adrian Fortescue and others who are bound with him to the King in 100 marks, call extremely upon him to save them harmless." June 9, 1533 (*Calendar, Henry VIII.* vol. 6, n. 611).

to the Crown by Lord Essex, for which he was being sued as one of his sureties, and he wrote on the same subject to Thomas Knyghton, Gent., dwelling at Bayford in Hertfordshire, signing it "with the hand of your old loving and acquainted friend, Adryan Fortescue, Kt." If April 17, 1539, as Sir Harris Nicolas gives it, were the correct date for Cromwell's elevation to the Earldrom of Essex, his predecessor in the title must have died before Sir Adrian. But Stowe and Wriothesley show plainly that Lord Essex died in the following year :

The 12th day of March, which was Friday before Passion Sunday, this year [1540] the Earl of Essex riding, a young horse by misfortune cast him and brake his neck at his place in Essex, which was great pity. This year also, the 19th day of March, the good Earl of Oxford [Sir John de Vere] died at his manor in Essex, which Earl was High Chamberlain of England.[28]

Hence it follows that Cromwell was not made Earl of Essex and High Chamberlain in 1539, but in 1540. It might well have been thought to have been the earlier year, for it seems almost incredible that his Act of Attainder should have been passed just two months after his elevation to the peerage. The attainder of Cromwell for heresy and treason was unanimously passed by Parliament on the 19th of June, and he was beheaded on the 28th of July, 1540.

To return to 1539, and Sir Adrian Fortescue. It must have been on the 14th of February that he was sent to the Tower, for a letter to Arthur Plantagenet Viscount Lisle, from a servant of his, named John Husee, dated[29] the 17th, says that "within these three days Sir Adrian Fortescue has been committed to the Tower and shall lose his head." On the 18th an Inventory was made of all his furniture, as well of his house at Brightwell, as of his "lodging beside the Black Friars in London." On the 28th of June, that is between his attainder and his death, his plate was seized by the King, and it is entered by John Williams, Master and Treasurer of his Grace's jewels, in the list of plate received for his Majesty's use from divers and sundry surrendered monasteries. It consisted of two basons and two ewers parcel gilt, weighing 164 *oz.* and two pots parcel gilt, weighing 84 *oz.* The family must have succeeded in saving the greater part of Sir Adrian's plate and other property from confiscation.

[28] Wriothesley's *Chronicle*, Camden Society, 1875, p. 113.
[29] The *Calendar, Henry VIII.* vol. 8, n. 231, places this letter in 1535.

Parliament met at Westminster on Monday, April 28, 1539. The work that Henry and Cromwell, his Vicar-General in spiritualities, wanted of it was the suppression of the greater monasteries, and this work it performed. It was therefore the last Parliament in which the Abbots sat as Peers. In this Parliament an entirely new proceeding was introduced, by which sentence of death might be passed, without any trial of the person accused, without evidence or any defence. Sir Thomas Gaudy, himself a Judge, told Sir Edward Coke that Cromwell sent for the Judges and asked them whether Parliament had the power to condemn persons without a hearing; and that the Judges answered that it was a nice and a dangerous question, that equity, justice and all laws required that the accused should be heard; that, however, Parliament being the supreme court of the realm, from which there could be no appeal, the validity of their sentences, of what nature soever they were, could not be questioned. This was only saying, in other words, that the Parliament would therein commit an injustice for which it could not be called to account.

Of this proceeding Coke wrote: "Although I question not the power of the Parliament, for without doubt the attainder stands good in law, yet I say of this manner of proceeding, *auferat oblivio, si potest ; si non, utrumque silentium tegat.* For the more high and absolute the jurisdiction of any court is, the more just and honourable it ought to be in its proceedings, in order to give examples of justice to inferior courts." And even Bishop Burnet says that "these and other such Acts of Attainder were of a strange and an unheard of nature; it is a blemish never to be washed off, and which cannot be enough condemned, and it was a breach of the most sacred and unalterable rules of justice never to be excused."

This Parliament, which suppressed the religious houses and passed the Six Articles, the most servile Parliament that ever sat in England, adopted at Cromwell's bidding the device by which Cromwell himself just a year later was condemned unheard. Margaret, Countess of Salisbury, first cousin to the King's mother, her son, Reginald Cardinal Pole, styled "one Reginald Pole, late Dean of Exeter," Gertrude [30] the widow of the recently executed Marquess of Exeter, Sir Adrian Fortescue and Sir Thomas Dingley, were with some others attainted of high treason without trial. The accusation against the Blessed

[30] Her attainder was reversed in Mary's first Parliament.

Margaret was that certain Bulls from Rome were found at Cowdray, Lord Southampton's house, where she had been detained as a prisoner ; that she kept up correspondence with her son the Cardinal, and that she forbade her tenants to have the New Testament in English in their houses. For all evidence on the day of the third reading of the Bill of Attainder, Cromwell, the Vicar-General stood up in the house and showed openly a certain habit, made of white silk, which was found by the Lord Admiral in the linen wardrobe of the Countess of Salisbury, on the forepart of which was embroidered the arms of England, and on the back part of it was the device of the Five Wounds of our Saviour, the Blessed Sacrament, and I.H.S. in the midst.

On the Parliamentary Roll is the attainder of Adrian Fortescue of Brightwell, Oxon, for sedition,[31] and that of Sir Thomas Dingley, Knight of St.John of Jerusalem, with Robert Granceter, merchant, for going to several foreign princes and persuading them to make war with the King. Sir Adrian and Hugh Vaughan of Bekener, who is mentioned on the Roll with the Countess of Salisbury were condemned as "confederates of the above." The "above," besides those mentioned, include Nicholas Throgmorton, John Helyard, clerk, Thomas Goldwell, clerk,[32] William Peto of West Greenwich, Observant, who have not only "adhered themselves to the Bishop of Rome," but "have taken and perceived worldly promotions of the gift of the same Bishop of Rome," which was true certainly of Cardinal Pole, "and also stirred up the people against the King," which was true of none of them. The Bill of Attainder was brought in and read twice on the 10th of May, and the third time on the day following.

"The 8th of July," says John Stowe, "Griffith Clark, Vicar of Wandsworth, with his chaplain and his servant, and Friar Waire, were all four hanged and quartered at St. Thomas Waterings. The 10th of July Sir Adrian Fortescue and Thomas Dingley were beheaded." The Grey Friars Chronicle says that, on "the 9th day of July was beheaded at Tower Hill Master Foskew and Master Dyngle, Knights ; and that same day was

---

[31] *The Parliamentary History of England*, London, 1751, vol. 3, p. 141. Cobbett in his edition of this book has omitted all mention of Sir Adrian's attainder, but he relates it in his *State Trials*.

[32] I am not aware that it has ever been noticed that Thomas Goldwell, afterwards Bishop of St. Asaph, was attainted in his absence at this time. I can find no record of the reversal of that attainder by Parliament in Queen Mary's reign.

drawn to Tyburn two of their servants, and there hanged and quartered for treason." Charles Wriothesley, Windsor Herald, in his Chronicle, also gives the day as the 9th of July, and he too makes mention of the execution for treason of the two serving men. The Knights of St. John give the 8th of July as the day of the martyrdom, but Sander gives the same date as Stowe. Blessed Margaret Pole, the last of the line and name of the Plantagenets, was kept in the Tower for two years more by her cruel kinsman, and there her head was hacked off on May 27, 1541.

That the two Knights should have died by beheading instead of the frightful death with which English law punished high treason, can have been only by the King's having extended to them the "mercy" that he had shown to Sir Thomas More; which had caused Blessed Thomas to answer, "God forbid that the King should use any more such mercy unto any of my friends, and God bless all my posterity from such pardons." However it was a real mercy to be spared the horrors of Tyburn, though there was cruelty enough remaining in any form of death undeserved.

A third Knight of the Order of St. John was martyred in the same year with Blessed Margaret of Salisbury. "The 1st of July" [1541], says Stowe,[33] "Sir David Genson, Knight of the Rhodes, was drawn through Southwark to St. Thomas of Waterings and there executed for the Supremacy." Charles Wriothesley[34] writes as if he knew the Martyr's father, who was probably a well-known citizen of London, living on the Southwark side of the river. We may adopt his spelling of the name, especially as it agrees with that in the indictment. "The 12th day of July one of Mr. Gunston's sons, which was a Knight of the Rhodes, was drawn from the King's Bench to St. Thomas Waterings, and there hanged and quartered for treason." In Malta Sir David's name was softened into Gonson, which is the origin, no doubt, of the form given by Stowe. In the Council Book of the Order in Malta, on the 20th of March, 1533, the Grand Master and his Council "ordered that Brother David Gonson should have a vote in the English *langue*, notwithstanding the opposition of Brother Thomas Torne." And "on the 2nd of September, 1534, Brother David Gonson, Knight of the English *langue*, obtained licence to depart from the Convent and go to his native country."[35]   The martyr's indictment in Trinity Term, 1541, says that David Gunston had been abroad from the 10th of July, 1536, to the 20th of August, 1539, and that, during that time, at Malta, he had denied that the King was the Supreme Head of the Church of England, that he had said that his Highness was a heretic and all who maintained this title were heretics, and that those who said that no one might appeal to the Pope but that it was better to appeal to the King, were worse than Turks and Lutherans.   The date given by Wriothesley for Sir David Gunston's martyrdom, July 12, is probably correct.   Sir David was a prisoner in the Marshalsea ; and St. Thomas Waterings, the first stage on the ancient pilgrims' way to Canterbury, was the usual place of execution for Southwark.

The Cause of Sir Adrian Fortescue, Sir Thomas Dingley, and Sir David Gunston, has been introduced among the 261 Martyrs who have lately been honoured with the title of Venerable.   But it is hoped that at least Sir Adrian may soon be held entitled to rank with the 54 who are declared Blessed.   The Knights of his Order have always held him to be a Martyr, and as such they have honoured him. There are three pictures of him in the island of Malta, two of them in the Church of St. John's at Valletta, amongst the *Beati*, with the emblem of martyrdom, the palm ; the third in the Collegio di S. Paolo, at Rabato, with the proper glory of a *Beato*.   In a picture that existed at Madrid in 1621, of which an official description exists in Malta, he was drawn with a knife in his throat, and the inscription called him Blessed.   This portrait was in the Church of the College of St. George in that city, and the Rabato picture is believed to be drawn from it.   Two English priests, William Numan and Edward Messendin, the Agent of Douay College at Madrid (his true name was Madison),[36] who were present when a Public Notary described the picture, declared that the history of the

[35] I am indebted to my good friend Dr. A. A. Caruana for these interesting extracts from the Maltese official books :

" Eodem die (xx mensis Martii 1533 ab Inc.)   Audita requisitione fratris Davidis Gonson, R[everendissi]mus D[ominus] M[agnus] M[agister] et V[enerabile] C[oncilium], non obstante contradictione fratris Thomæ Torne, decreverunt quod habeat votum in veneranda lingua " (*Lib. Concil.* 1526—35, fol. 111).

"Die 2 mensis Septembris 1534, Frater David Gonson linguæ Angliæ miles obtinuit licentiam recedendi ex Conventu et eundi ad patriam in forma," etc. (*Lib. Bull.* 1531—34, fol. 168 t.).

[36] *Douay Diary*, p. 35.

aforesaid Knight and Martyr was related by Sander in the seventh book of his *De Visibili Monarchia.* A careful search in the book referred to, does not verify their assertion. When Nicholas Fortescue, in 1639, made application to Grand Master Lascaris to be received into the Order with the view of re-suscitating the English *langue,* he supported his petition by invoking " the memorials that are read in the chronicles, and the holiness of Blessed Adrian Fortescue, Knight of the Order, who is numbered amongst the Saints that are revered in the Oratory of the great Church of St. John."

In addition to the Missal that Sir Adrian has left behind him, we have already spoken of the other very interesting relic, which is now in the Bodleian library—the volume on the flyleaf of which is the record of his second son's birth and baptism. The whole book is in Sir Adrian's handwriting, as he himself notes in it twice over, with the date 1532. This was the year of his second marriage, and his wife has written her name on it, together with the name of her second husband, " Parry," showing that she retained possession of it after his execution. It passed into the hands of Sir Kenelm Digby, whose name is also written upon it.

Sir Adrian has written these interesting words on the first page :

JESUS.   JESUS.

Iste liber pertinet Adriano Fortescu militi, sua manu propria scriptus anno Dni. 1532, et anno R[egni] R[egis] Henr. VIII. xxiiij[to.]

Loyall Pensee.

Injuriarum remedium—Oblivio.

Omnium rerum vicissitudo.

Garde les portes de ta bouche,

Pour fouyr peryl et reproche.

The volume consists of the treatise *On Absolute and Limited Monarchy,* by his great-uncle, Chancellor Fortescue, preceded by a large part of the old poem of *Piers Plowman,* and at the end there is an ample collection of proverbs, from which we here make a selection.

> A king sekant [seeking] treason shall find it in his land.
> When the fault is in the head, the member is oft sick.
> Many [a] one glosses the law, oft against the poor.
> He, that ruleth well his tongue, is held for wise.
> Money gotten at the dice [en]richeth not the heir.
> A woman, if she be fair, may hap to be good.

It is easy to cry Yule[37] at another man's cost.
He shall hunger in frost that in heat will not work.
Eat and drink by measure, and defy thy leech.
Men of muckle speech must sometimes lie.
A man may be of good kin, and himself little worth.
Thou must trow [trust] some man, or have an ill life.
He that toucheth pitch and tar cannot long be clean.
A wound when it is green is best to be healed.
Unkindness by-past would be forgot.
For little more or less make no debate.
He that covets all is able all to tyne [lose].
About thine and mine riseth muckle strife.
He hath a blessed life that holds him content.
He that wots [knows] when he is full, is no fool.
Put many to school, all will not be clerks.
There is not so little a flea but sometime he will nye [annoy].
At every dog that barks one ought not to be annoyed.
He that is well loved, he is not poor.
A good tale, ill told, is spoilt in the telling.
He that wots when to leap will sometimes look aback.
Wherefore serves the lock, and the thief in the house?
It makes a wanton mouse, an unhardy cat.
A swine that is over fat is cause of his own death.

A few of the proverbs are religious, and we have kept them for the last.

Obey well the good Kirk and thou shalt fare the better.
Think ay thou shalt die, thou shalt not gladly sin.
Be blythe at thy meat, devout at thy Mass.[38]
He that dreads not God shall not fail to fall.

Lady Fortescue, the martyr's widow, was held in high favour by Queen Mary. She attended the Queen as she went in state on September 30, 1553, from the Tower to her palace at Westminster, and she is the first named of ten ladies "who rode in crimson velvet, their horses trapped with the same." Sir Adrian's daughter Margaret, Lady Wentworth, had a place in the same procession. In the fifth year of Queen Mary's reign, several manors in Gloucestershire were granted by the Crown to "Anne Fortescue, widow of Sir Adrian Fortescue, and to the

---

[37] "In Yorkshire and our other northern parts, they have an old custom after sermon or service on Christmas Day, the people will, even in the churches, cry *Ule, ule,* as a token of rejoicing" (Blount, quoted by Halliwell).
[38] This reminds us of the grand old Catholic proverb : Meat and Mass hinder no man.

heirs male of Sir Adrian." It is singular that she should be called in the grants by the name of Fortescue, for she was already married to Sir Thomas Ap-harry, or Parry. Her second husband was a Protestant, and was sworn of the Privy Council by Queen Elizabeth at the first Council held after her accession. He had been "a servant much about her" as Princess Elizabeth, and she at once made him Comptroller of her Household.

Sir Adrian's "little son John" was a boy of eight at the time of his father's death, born in the same year as Queen Elizabeth. He was brought up a Protestant, and his father's attainder was reversed in 1552 in his favour in the reign of Edward the Sixth. He was soon after chosen to be preceptor to the Princess Elizabeth, and when she became Queen she made him Keeper of the Great Wardrobe. In 1591 he was made Chancellor of the Exchequer, and when he died in 1607, having outlived Elizabeth, he was Chancellor of the Duchy of Lancaster. He acquired the manor of Salden, Bucks, from his step-father, Sir Thomas Parry, and he was the founder of the Salden branch of the Fortescue family, which became extinct in the male line in 1729, but in the female line is now represented by the Turvilles and the Amhersts.

One has but to look at the portrait of Sir John Fortescue to feel sure that he was a Protestant. And no one would have doubted it, if Father Tesimond, in his narrative[39] of his landing in England, had not given a circumstantial account of his having gone straight to the house of Sir John Fortescue, Keeper of the Queen's Wardrobe, at a most inopportune moment, when the whole house had been upset the night before by pursuivants in search of priests. He further says that two or three priests had concealed themselves in hiding-places, that the pursuivants had carried away books, pictures, vestments, and altar furniture, and that Sir John himself together with his wife and children were in custody, among them "two little girls, the fairest in London." "They greatly feared that Sir John would lose his office of Keeper of the Wardrobe, and in point of fact, some time after, he did lose it, though not on that occasion, as he had many friends and relations at Court." This was at the end of 1597 or early in 1598.

But it is clear, on a careful examination, that Father Tesimond has confused together two John Fortescues, and the house to which he went on his arrival in England was that of

[39] *Troubles of our Catholic Forefathers,* First Series, p. 174.

John Fortescue, who was a nephew of Sir John, the Master of the Queen's Wardrobe. The younger John Fortescue was the son of Sir Anthony, the third son of Sir Adrian and of Catherine daughter of Sir Geoffrey Pole, the brother of the Cardinal, unattainted because he had turned against and betrayed his own flesh and blood. However, John Fortescue was proud that "his mother was niece to Cardinal Pole." He lived in London, with his wife Helen, and "their house was a receptacle for all priests and Religious men without partiality or exception." The two daughters, Catherine and Elizabeth, "the fairest girls in London," married, the one Francis Bedingfeld, and had eleven daughters who all became nuns, and the other Sir John Beaumont of Gracedieu. This John Fortescue had no doubt "many friends and relations at Court," of whom his uncle, the Chancellor of the Exchequer, was the most powerful. His father, Sir Anthony, could not help him, for he was himself attainted, if not at that time a prisoner in the Tower for conspiring against the Queen with Arthur and Edward Pole. But his grandmother, Anne Lady Parry, could have said a good word for him, as she was now as high in the favour of Elizabeth as she had been in that of Queen Mary.

A letter from John Fortescue to the Earl of Essex on the occasion of the very arrest described by Father Tesimond is given by Lord Clermont from the Hatfield collection of manuscripts. In it he tries to exculpate himself by saying, "I crave no favour of her Majesty or any peer within this realm, if any unnatural or disloyal fact can be proved against me either in harbouring, maintaining or abetting either priest or Jesuit, forbidden by her Highness' laws." "And in this search at my house," he goes on to say, "myself being then in the country, there was nothing found within my command in all my house, but such things as my lewd and wretched butler had locked in a desk of his in that office, so far from my knowledge (on my salvation) as is heaven from earth." He then says that he has served her Majesty these twenty-one years and has "never been touched with any blot of such disorder," and it was not likely that he would deprive himself of that benefit which had maintained himself his wife and children these many years. And then he adds this curious sentence: "and in which space, if I have retained my conscience at all, her Majesty hath been no loser by it, nor myself, God knoweth any great gainer." This letter is dated March 8, 1597, which being O.S. shows that Father

Tesimond's arrival was in March, 1598, N.S. The house we learn was in Black Friars; at least so it is said in a paper which Lord Clermont has found at Ushaw, in which, after the deaths at St. Omers of both John Fortescue and his wife Helen, an account is given of how Father John Gerard besought Mrs. Fortescue to let him have a lodging in her house in which he might privately meet Catesby, Percy, Winter, Digby, and others who were afterwards implicated in the Gunpowder Plot; and how, after the discovery of the Plot, Father Gerard suddenly appeared at Mr. Fortescue's house, disguised by a false beard and hair, and asked to be taken in as he knew not where to hide his head, on which Mr. Fortescue much grieved, looked at him and said, "Have you no one to ruin but me and my family?" This paper was written with an unhappy desire of making the Jesuits responsible for the Gunpowder Plot.

It must have seemed that the main line of the Fortescues of Salden was irretrievably lost to the Church. Sir Francis, son and heir of Sir John, was made a Knight of the Bath at the coronation of James I. But yet, during his father's lifetime Francis is described by Father John Gerard[40] as "a Catholic by conviction, but conforming externally to the State religion for fear of offending his father." His wife, Grace Manners, Father Gerard converted, but though her husband Sir Francis "made no difficulty of receiving priests, and at last went so far as to be fond of dressing the altar with his own hands and of saying the breviary, yet with all this he remains outside the ark," wrote Father Gerard in 1609, "for he presumes too much on an opportunity of doing penance before death." Father Anthony Hoskins was their first resident priest, and Salden continued to be a Jesuit mission even after it had ceased to belong to the Fortescues. It is very singular that no trace of the fact that this branch of the family was Catholic should have reached Lord Clermont when he was compiling his admirable and most painstaking family history. Adrian Fortescue, the great-grandson of our martyr, was a Jesuit, and Sir Francis, the fourth baronet, in whom the male line expired, was at one time a Novice in the Society.

<hr />

[40] *Life of Father John Gerard*, p. 335.

www.ingramcontent.com/pod-product-compliance
Lightning Source LLC
Chambersburg PA
CBHW031931060726
47496CB00009BA/2922